I AM BRAVE

勇敢做自己

胡媛媛 编

广东旅游出版社
GUANGDONG TRAVEL & TOURISM PRESS
中国·广州

图书在版编目（ＣＩＰ）数据

勇敢做自己 / 胡媛媛编. — 广州：广东旅游出版社，2016.11
（儿童情绪管理与性格培养绘本）
ISBN 978-7-5570-0548-1

Ⅰ.①勇… Ⅱ.①胡… Ⅲ.①儿童故事 – 图画故事 – 中国 – 当代 Ⅳ.①I287.8

中国版本图书馆 CIP 数据核字(2016)第 237814 号

总 策 划：罗艳辉
责任编辑：殷如筠
封面绘图：赵里骏
责任技编：刘振华
责任校对：李瑞苑

勇 敢 做 自 己
YONGGAN ZUO ZIJI

广东旅游出版社出版发行
（广州市越秀区建设街道环市东路 338 号银政大厦西楼 12 楼　邮编：510030）
邮购电话：020–87348243
广东旅游出版社图书网
www.tourpress.cn
湖北楚天传媒印务有限责任公司
（湖北省武汉市东湖新技术开发区流芳园横路 1 号　邮编：430205）
787 毫米×1092 毫米　16 开　2 印张　1 千字
2016 年 11 月第 1 版第 1 次印刷
定价：15.00 元

晚上,兔爸爸和兔妈妈出门了,留小兔独自在家。

In the evening, father rabbit and mother rabbit went out and left Rabbit home alone.

小兔一边玩玩具，一边自言自语地说："爸爸妈妈怎么还没回来呢？"

Rabbit was playing toys and said to herself, "when will Mom and Dad come home?"

小兔有点儿害怕了，心"怦怦"跳个不停。"我要做一个勇敢的孩子。"她边整理玩具边为自己打气。

Rabbit's heart was thumping with fear. "I want to be a brave child," she tidied her toys and encouraged herself.

　　这时，窗帘轻轻抖了几下。"是不是大灰狼来了？"小兔害怕极了。

　　　Suddenly, the curtain flapped. "Is the wolf coming?" Rabbit was very scared.

嘀嗒……嘀嗒……"这是大灰狼的心跳声吗？"小兔赶紧跳上床，躲进被子里。

Tick tock, tick tock. "Is that the wolf's heartbeat?" Rabbit jumped onto the bed quickly and covered herself with the quilt.

门外传来一阵窸窸窣窣的声音。"是大灰狼要闯进来吗？"小兔偷偷把被子掀开一丝缝，睁大眼睛。

She heard something rustling out of the door. "Is the wolf going to intrude into the house?" Rabbit opened the quilt a little and looked from the crack carefully.

"啊，是爸爸妈妈回来了！"小兔高兴地跳下床，扑到妈妈怀里。

"Oh, Dad and Mom came home!" Rabbit jumped out of the bed happily and jumped into her mom's arms.

爸爸摸着小兔的脑袋问："刚才躲在被子里，准备吓唬我们吗？"

"不。窗户那儿有大灰狼！"

Father rabbit stroked Rabbit's head and asked, "you was hiding in the quilt. You wanted to scare us, right?"
"No. There is a wolf outside the window!"

爸爸走到窗户前，一把掀开了窗帘，可是窗外什么也没有。

Father rabbit went to the window and opened the curtain, but nothing was there.

"可是刚才窗帘真的一动一动的！" 小兔委屈地说。

"But the curtain was really flapping!" Rabbit said sadly.

窗帘又飘动起来。"原来是调皮的风弟弟。"小兔红着脸，低下了头。

The curtain flapped again. "Oh, it was a naughty wind." Rabbit blushed and lowered head.

"我还听见了'嘀嗒、嘀嗒'的声音，那一定是大灰狼的心跳。"小兔坚定地说。

"I also heard ticking. It must be the wolf's heartbeat," Rabbit said firmly.

妈妈从桌上拿起小闹钟，放在小兔的耳边，"嘀嗒嘀嗒"的声音听得很清楚。小兔的脸更红了。

Mother rabbit took the clock from the table and placed it to Rabbit's ear. Tick tock, tick tock. It could be heard clearly. Rabbit blushed again.

"说出自己的害怕就很勇敢啊！"
爸爸笑眯眯地抱起小兔。

"But you are so brave to speak out your fear!" Father rabbit held Rabbit in arm with a smile.

"愿意面对自己的害怕更加勇敢！"妈妈竖起大拇指。

"It is braver to face up to your fear!" Mother rabbit gave her a thumbs up.

不一会儿，小兔躺在床上睡着了。

After a while, Rabbit fell asleep.

在梦中，小兔变得非常高大，还把凶狠的大灰狼给赶跑了！

In her dream, Rabbit became tall and big. She drove a fierce wolf away.

第二天早晨，小兔挺着小胸脯对爸爸妈妈说："我再也不害怕大灰狼了，我要做最勇敢的自己！"

Rabbit held her head up and said to her mom and dad the next morning, "I no longer fear the wolf. I will be the bravest!"

给父母的话：

　　现如今，在爷爷奶奶、爸爸妈妈等众多长辈的过度关爱和保护下，很多小朋友都变得胆小怯懦，遇事害怕逃避。其实，每个父母都希望自己的孩子勇敢有担当。但怎样才能培养孩子勇敢的精神呢？

　　首先，理解孩子的感受。当孩子表现出胆小和畏缩心理，我们应该站在孩子的立场去理解孩子，安慰孩子，让他们能够从容地面对内心的害怕，进而克服恐惧心理，变得勇敢起来。其次，帮助孩子正确认知。有时候，孩子不了解或不能正确认识自己所害怕的对象，导致了其不合理的恐惧心理。就像文中的小兔那样，偶有风吹草动就惊惧不已。这时父母应该像小兔的爸爸妈妈那样，引导孩子了解信息，纠正其错误想法，树立正确的认知，这样可以减轻或消除孩子的恐惧心理，让孩子变得大胆起来。再次，鼓励孩子，培养自信。如果孩子缺少自信，就容易对环境产生怀疑与戒备。而当孩子有了自信，就会更勇敢地去面对未知的恐惧和困难。自信的孩子往往也是勇敢的孩子。最后，父母要以身作则，树立榜样。怯懦的父母教不出勇敢的孩子。父母应该用自己的实际言行告诉孩子，胆小于事无补，勇往直前才能解决问题。另外可以给孩子讲一些勇敢者的事迹，激发孩子对于勇敢精神的向往。